Tadpoles
Fairytale Twists

Snow White
Sees the Light

Written by Karen Wallace
Illustrated by Andy Rowland

Crabtree Publishing Company
www.crabtreebooks.com

Crabtree Publishing Company
www.crabtreebooks.com
1-800-387-7650

616 Welland Ave.
St. Catharines, ON
L2M 5V6

PMB 59051, 350 Fifth Ave.
59th Floor,
New York, NY 10118

Published by Crabtree Publishing in 2015

Series editor: Melanie Palmer
Editor: Kathy Middleton
Proofreader: Shannon Welbourn
Notes to adults: Reagan Miller
Series advisor: Catherine Glavina
Series designer: Peter Scoulding
Production coordinator and
    Prepress technician: Margaret Amy Salter
Print coordinator: Katherine Berti

Text © Karen Wallace 2012
Illustrations © Andy Rowland 2012

The rights of Karen Wallace
to be identified as the author
and Andy Rowland as the
illustrator of this Work have
been asserted.

First published in 2012
by Franklin Watts
(A division of Hachette
Children's Books)

Printed in
Canada/022015/IH20141209

**Library and Archives Canada
Cataloguing in Publication**

Wallace, Karen, author
     Snow White sees the light / written by Karen
Wallace ; illustrated by Andy Rowland.

(Tadpoles: fairytale twists)
Originally published in 2012.
Issued in print and electronic formats.
ISBN 978-0-7787-1931-1 (bound).--
ISBN 978-0-7787-1957-1 (pbk.).--
ISBN 978-1-4271-7695-0 (pdf).--
ISBN 978-1-4271-7687-5 (html)

     I. Rowland, Andrew, 1962-, illustrator II.
Title. III. Series: Tadpoles. Fairytale twists

PZ7.W158Sn 2015   j823'.92   C2014-907775-0
                                            C2014-907776-9

**Library of Congress
Cataloging-in-Publication Data**

CIP available at Library of Congress

This story is based on the traditional fairy tale,
Snow White and the Seven Dwarfs, but with a new twist.
Can you make up your own twist for the story?

Snow White put down
her broom and sighed.

Every day the seven dwarfs left
muddy boots in the kitchen and
dropped their jackets on the floor.

5

They never took off their hats.

They only wanted to be fed.

"What's cooking?"

"I'm starving!"

"Hurry up!"

When they sat at the table, the dwarfs had terrible manners.

And they never ever cleared
the table or helped wash
the dishes!

One day, Snow White lost her temper. "All you want is a housekeeper," she cried. "You don't care about me!"

The dwarfs stared at her
in amazement.

11

"But we adore you," said one.

"You are the loveliest in the land," cried another.

"We'd be lost without you!" said a third.

"Ha!" cried Snow White.
But she went to put a pie in
the oven anyway.

Far away, a wise queen lived in a castle. She believed that everyone in her kingdom should share the cooking and cleaning.

That way everyone
would be happy.

15

One day, the queen picked up
her magic mirror.
"Mirror, mirror in my hand, does
someone need me in my land?"

"Snow White needs you," replied
the mirror right away.
"The seven dwarfs are treating
her like a slave."

The queen visited Snow White. "Why do you let the dwarfs get away with it?" she asked.

"They say they'd be lost without me," replied Snow White.

"We'll see about that," said the queen. She cut a piece out of a magic apple.

"Pretend you've been poisoned
and see what the dwarfs say when
they find you."

That evening, the seven dwarfs marched in the door, kicked off their boots, and shouted for their supper.

Then they saw Snow White
lying on the floor with the
apple beside her.

"Oh, no!" cried the dwarfs. "That apple is poisoned! Snow White is dead!" They all burst into tears.

"Who's going to cook our food?"

"Who's going to clean our house?"

"Who's going to wash our clothes?"

Snow White got up from the floor
and gave the seven dwarfs
a long, hard stare.

"Wash your own clothes!" she said.
"I'm leaving!"

And guess what? Snow White found a nice, considerate prince and lived very happily ever after.

Puzzle 1

Put these pictures in the correct order. Which event do you think is the most important? Now try writing the story in your own words!

Puzzle 2

Choose the correct speech bubbles for each character. Can you think of any others? Turn the page to find the answers for both pages.

Notes for adults

TADPOLES: Fairytale Twists are engaging, imaginative stories designed for early fluent readers. The books may also be used for read-alouds or shared reading with young children.

TADPOLES: Fairytale Twists are humorous stories with a unique twist on traditional fairy tales. Each story can be compared to the original fairy tale, or appreciated on its own. Fairy tales are a key type of literary text found in the Common Core State Standards.

THE FOLLOWING PROMPTS BEFORE, DURING, AND AFTER READING SUPPORT LITERACY SKILL DEVELOPMENT AND CAN ENRICH SHARED READING EXPERIENCES:

1. **Before Reading**: Do a picture walk through the book, previewing the illustrations. Ask the reader to predict what will happen in the story. For example, ask the reader what he or she thinks the twist in the story will be.

2. **During Reading**: Encourage the reader to use context clues and illustrations to determine the meaning of unknown words or phrases.

3. **During Reading**: Have the reader stop midway through the book to revisit his or her predictions. Does the reader wish to change his or her predictions based on what they have read so far?

4. **During and After Reading**: Encourage the reader to make different connections:
   Text-to-Text: How is this story similar to/different from other stories you have read?
   Text-to-World: How are events in this story similar to/different from things that happen in the real world?
   Text-to-Self: Does a character or event in this story remind you of anything in your own life?

5. **After Reading**: Encourage the child to reread the story and to retell it using his or her own words. Invite the child to use the illustrations as a guide.

HERE ARE OTHER TITLES FROM TADPOLES: FAIRYTALE TWISTS FOR YOU TO ENJOY:

Cinderella's Big Foot	978-0-7787-0440-9 RLB	978-0-7787-0448-5 PB
Hansel and Gretel and the Green Witch	978-0-7787-1928-1 RLB	978-0-7787-1954-0 PB
Jack and the Bean Pie	978-0-7787-0441-6 RLB	978-0-7787-0449-2 PB
Little Bad Riding Hood	978-0-7787-0442-3 RLB	978-0-7787-0450-8 PB
Princess Frog	978-0-7787-0443-0 RLB	978-0-7787-0452-2 PB
Rapunzel and the Prince of Pop	978-0-7787-1929-8 RLB	978-0-7787-1955-7 PB
Rumpled Stilton Skin	978-0-7787-1930-4 RLB	978-0-7787-1956-4 PB
Sleeping Beauty—100 Years Later	978-0-7787-0444-7 RLB	978-0-7787-0479-9 PB
The Elves and the Trendy Shoes	978-0-7787-1932-8 RLB	978-0-7787-1958-8 PB
The Emperor's New Uniform	978-0-7787-1933-5 RLB	978-0-7787-1959-5 PB
The Lovely Duckling	978-0-7787-0445-4 RLB	978-0-7787-0480-5 PB
The Pied Piper and the Wrong Song	978-0-7787-1934-2 RLB	978-0-7787-1960-1 PB
The Princess and the Frozen Peas	978-0-7787-0446-1 RLB	978-0-7787-0481-2 PB
The Three Frilly Goats Fluff	978-0-7787-1935-9 RLB	978-0-7787-1961-8 PB
The Three Little Pigs and the New Neighbor	978-0-7787-0447-8 RLB	978-0-7787-0482-9 PB

VISIT WWW.CRABTREEBOOKS.COM FOR OTHER CRABTREE BOOKS.

Answers
Puzzle 1
The correct order is: 1f, 2d, 3e, 4a, 5c, 6b
Puzzle 2
Snow White: 2, 3; The queen: 1, 4
The seven dwarfs: 5, 6